This book is for:

_____

from:

_____

Dedication

For Tom and Beth,
my fantastic parents.

A SLUGS & BUGS STORY

Are We Still Friends?

RANDALL GOODGAME

illustrated by Cory Jones

B&H kids

Nashville TN

Hip hip hooray for picnic day!
A time for food and fun

with Doug and Sparky, grizzly bears, raccoons, and everyone!

Sparky asked, "What's in the sack?"
"Here, take a look," Doug said.
"Dandelions, raisins, and some
pumpernickel bread."

"Cool! I've got a peanut butter
sandwich, carrots, aaaand . . .

a bag of Flavor-Blasted
Pizza Chips from Pizzaland!"

"Flavor-Blasted Pizza Chips!?
I love those chips
so much!"

"Me too," said Sparky. "Pizzaland has got the magic touch."

Then Maggie the Raccoon
walked up, a twinkle in her jaw,
twiddling a purple ping-pong
paddle in her paw,

"Do you know what time it is?"
she riddled right at Doug.
"It's time for my rematch with
your friend the lightning bug!"

Sparky clapped—"Of course!
we planned to play on picnic day!
I'll be right back, Doug,
once I put this sly raccoon away."

Sparky kidded Maggie,
but she answered with a rhyme,

"You're going down
like a frown
on a clown *this* time!"

So Sparky went with Maggie,
but Doug was not alone,
for right there on the table,
making his poor stomach groan…

was the brand-new bag of pizza chips!
Doug's very favorite kind.
So he thought, *I'll just eat one.
I know my friend won't mind.*

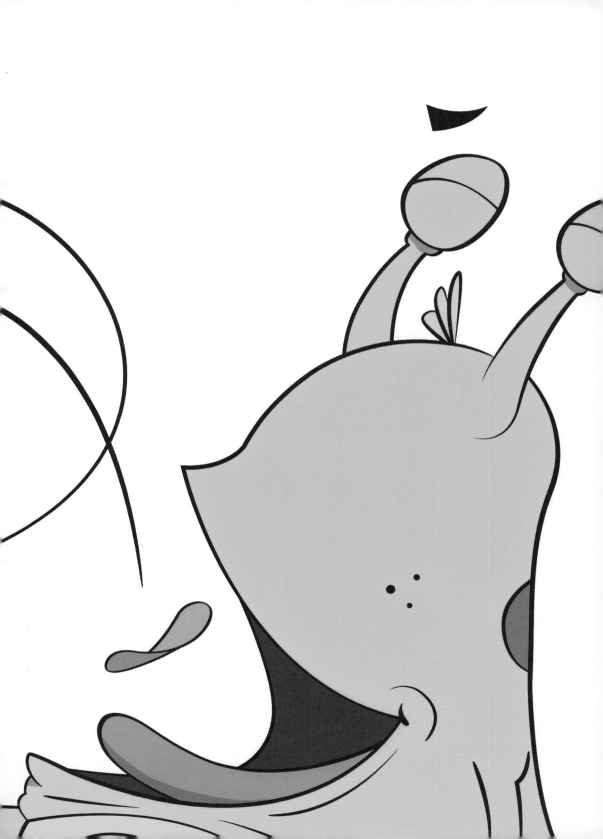

"Mmmm, that's TASTY!

Sparky is so nice to share with me."

Just one more, Doug thought.

But he took two,

and that makes three.

Then a mantis waved a canvas.
That was strange . . . and nice.
But it distracted Doug, and then
he gobbled *more* chips—twice!

A charm of hummingbirds flew by and spilled a couple (crunch).

A grizzly with a whizbee
made the table tremble (munch).

Doug kept chomping,
watching poky turtles playing tag.

Then he felt the crinkle
of the bottom
of the bag.

"The chips! GUAYAAAGH!!"
Doug gasped and groaned,
"Oh no! What have I done?
My fingertips are flavor blasted!
And now here they come!"

The ping-pong pair
approached their friend.
"Hey, Doug! Is something wrong?"

Doug hid his hands.
"Uh . . . Sparky,
all your pizza chips are gone!"

"What happened?" Sparky asked.
"Did someone take them from the table?"
(And now, dear friends, the saddest
moment in this happy fable . . .)

Doug knew what he had done,
but he did *not* want to admit it.
So he told a lie. "Um . . . yes,"
Doug said. "Someone *else* did it."

"Who was it?" Maggie asked.
"Maybe they did it for a laugh."

Since one lie
      always makes another,
            Doug said, "A . . . giraffe?"

Then Jane Giraffe looked in and said,
"Oh, heavens!" and "Good grief!
Let me ask my friends, and then
I'm sure we'll find the thief."

"NO! WAIT!" Doug said.

"No, not a giraffe. A camel did it!"

Then Karen Camel piped up.

"I'll ask Pam. Maybe she hid it!"

"HOLD ON, Karen.

Maybe it was not a camel either.

I remember now, it was . . . a . . .

bearded ancient

beaver!"

An ancient beaver croaked out,
"You should check my beard
for crumbs!"

But Sparky said, "Doug . . .
what's that on your fingers
and your thumbs?"

And when they saw his orange hands,
the crowd went cricket-quiet.
Someone whistled long and low.
Doug sighed. "I can't deny it."

"It was *me*.

I'm sorry, ancient beaver.

Sorry, camel.

I ate the chips!

It wasn't a giraffe

or any mammal.

"I didn't mean to eat them all
and wreck our picnic trip.
But it was me. I ate them—
every last, delicious chip."

"I'm so sorry, Sparky.

They were gone before I knew it."

Softly, Sparky said,

"Of course you didn't mean to do it."

The crowd gur-rumphed
and grumbled
as Doug fumbled what to say.

But as his mumble
stumbled ...
Sparky turned and
walked away.

Then everybody left,
except for Maggie, the raccoon.
She said, "Go talk to your friend,
but this time sing a different tune.

"He's not mad about the chips.
He's hurt because you lied.
A friendship isn't real
if you can't trust the other side."

Doug found his friend
folded on a stump and looking glum.
"I'm sorry that I lied to you,"
he said. "That was so dumb."

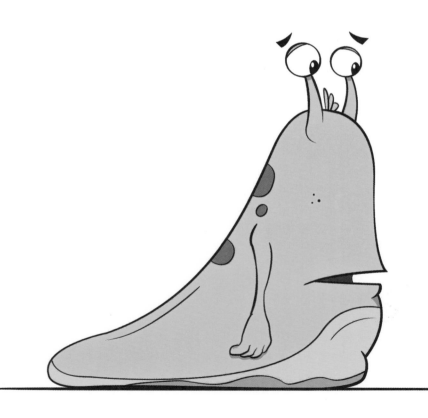

Sparky answered, "I picked out those chips because of you. I know how much you like them, and that makes *me* happy too."

"Are we still friends?" Doug asked.

"Or should we sort of wait and see?"

And Sparky said, "I hope so. . . .
I mean . . . I would like to be.

"I forgive you, Doug.
Sometimes it's hard to be a friend.
And everybody gets it wrong-ways
every now and then."

"And who else could I ever play invisible submarine with?

And how else could we ever play leviathan and behemoth!?"

"And who else makes me laugh like a hyena with no fleas?"

Then suddenly they heard a "Yoo-hoo!" way up in the trees. . . .

It was Jane Giraffe! And they could not believe their eyes.

She had a bag of pizza chips, giraffe-gigantic size!

She passed the massive bag to Sparky.

"Thank you, Jane!" Doug cried.

And they feasted on the pizza chips

till they were satisfied.

Then the afternoon unfolded
like a blanket on the lawn,

Filling picnic day with fun,
long after all the chips were gone.

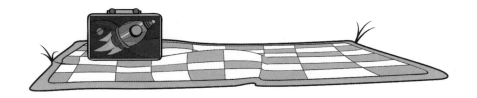

Be kind and compassionate to one
another, forgiving each other, just
as in Christ God forgave you.
—Ephesians 4:32